# ANNIE'S CAT IS SAD

**HEATHER SMITH**

illustrated by **KAREN OBUHANYCH**

Feiwel and Friends
New York

Hi, Delilah.
Did you miss me?
I missed you.

Are you okay?
You look sad.
Did you have a bad day?
Do you need a hug?

Delilah? Where are you going?

Delilah! Come back!

It's okay.
I get it.
You need some alone time.

I'll just sit here and wait.

Delilah? I made you some warm milk.
Not interested? What if I call it a cattuccino?

Don't worry.

I understand.

Nothing seems funny
when you've had a bad day.

Not even a cat pun.

Are you sure you don't need a hug?
I know when I've had a bad day, a hug helps.

By the way, I drank your cattuccino.
I wasn't going to, but I'm glad I did.
It made me feel warm.

How about some TV?
TV might cheer you up.

You should have watched that cartoon, Delilah.

It would have helped you forget about your bad day.

For a little while, anyway.

How about some exercise?
I heard yoga helps.

Look—
downward dog!

And . . . um . . .

upward unicorn!

And . . . uh . . .
flailing fish!

That was fun.

For a while there, I forgot
you were having a bad day.

Delilah?

A word of warning—
Just when you think you've forgotten your
bad day, you will remember it again.

I just want you to know.
It's okay to cry.

I knew a hug would make you feel better.

FOR KALI —H. S.
FOR MY GIRLS, ARIA AND CRACKERS —K. O.

A FEIWEL AND FRIENDS BOOK
An imprint of Macmillan Publishing Group, LLC
120 Broadway, New York, NY 10271 · mackids.com

Our books may be purchased in bulk for promotional, educational, or business use.
Please contact your local bookseller or the Macmillan Corporate and Premium Sales Department
at (800) 221-7945 ext. 5442 or by email at MacmillanSpecialMarkets@macmillan.com.

Library of Congress Cataloging-in-Publication Data is available.

First edition, 2022
Book design by Ashley Caswell
Acrylic paint, colored pencils, paper collage,
watercolor, and digital tools.
Feiwel and Friends logo designed by Filomena Tuosto
Printed in China by RR Donnelley Asia Printing Solutions Ltd.,
Dongguan City, Guangdong Province

ISBN 978-1-250-80684-0 (hardcover)
10 9 8 7 6 5 4 3 2 1